Little Wolf,
Pack Leader

Also by Ian Whybrow
and illustrated by Tony Ross

Little Wolf's Book of Badness
Little Wolf's Diary of Daring Deeds
Little Wolf's Haunted Hall for Small Horrors
Little Wolf, Forest Detective
Little Wolf's Postbag
Little Wolf's Handy Book of Peoms

Little Wolf's website address is:
www.littlewolf.co.uk

First published in Great Britain by Collins in 2002
Collins is an imprint of HarperCollins*Publishers* Ltd
77-85 Fulham Palace Road, Hammersmith, London W6 8JB

The HarperCollins website address is www.**fire**and**water**.com

3 5 7 9 8 6 4 2

Text copyright © 2002 Ian Whybrow
Illustrations copyright © 2002 Tony Ross

ISBN 0 00 711860 0

The author and illustrator assert the moral right to be
identified as the author and illustrator of the work.

Printed and bound in England by
Clays Ltd, St Ives plc

Little Wolf,
Pack Leader

Ian Whybrow

Illustrated by Tony Ross

Collins

An imprint of HarperCollinsPublishers

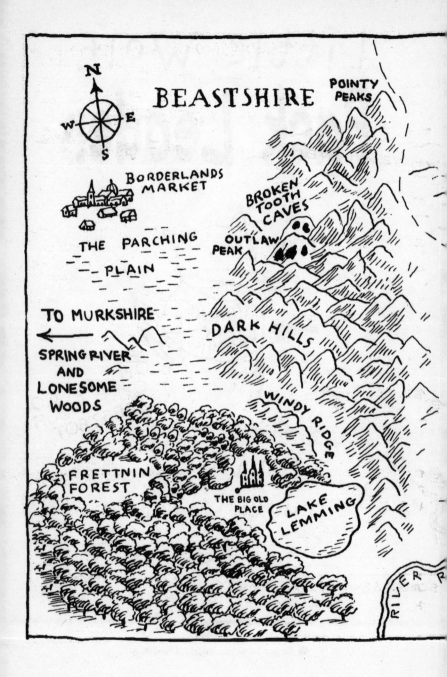

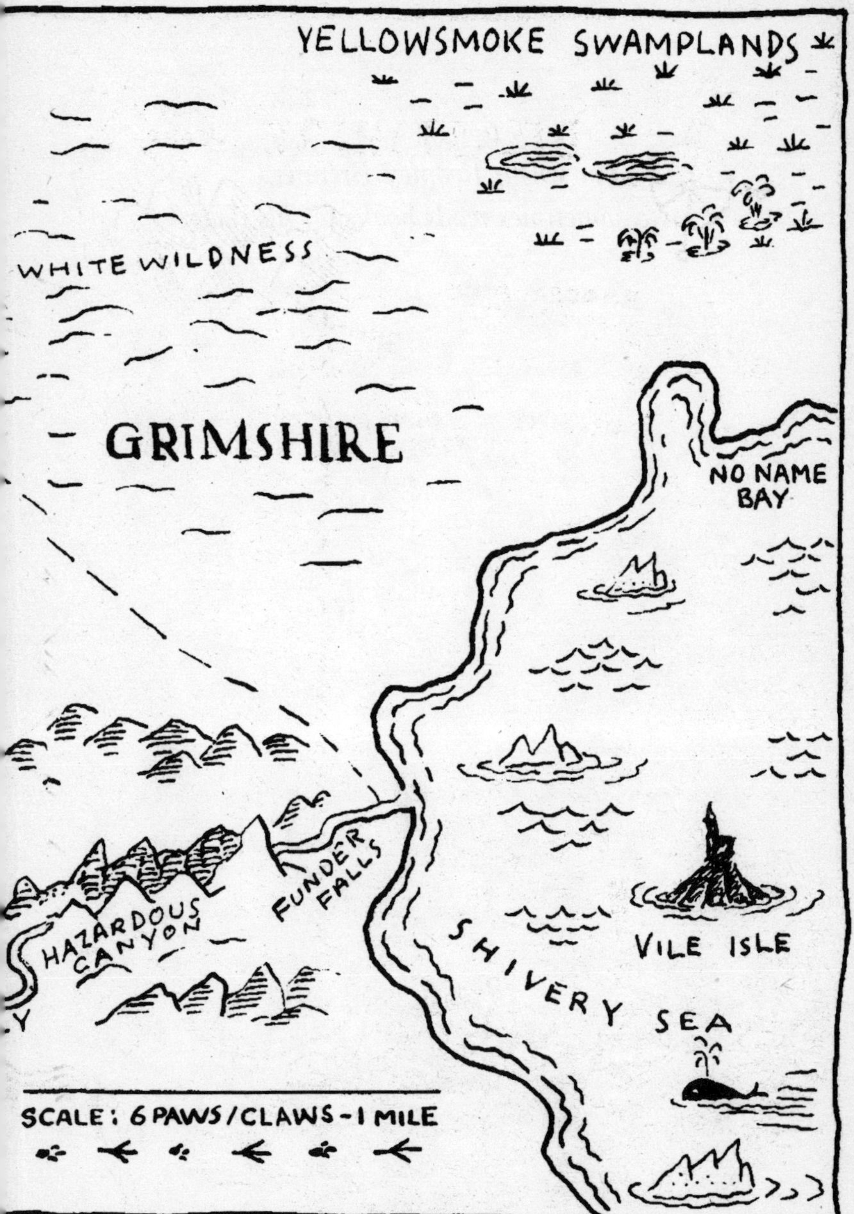
YELLOWSMOKE SWAMPLANDS
WHITE WILDNESS
GRIMSHIRE
NO NAME BAY
FUNDER FALLS
HAZARDOUS CANYON
VILE ISLE
SHIVERY SEA
SCALE: 6 PAWS/CLAWS - 1 MILE

For Oisín Twomey Brenner,
who sometimes reads books for his dad

Dear Mum and Dad,

You say in your letter how is our darling baby pet,
hmmm? I am kwite well thank you for not asking,
hem hem, I know you mean Smellybreff really.

Answer, Smells is his usual small painy self.
He has got a new craze, it is being a pop star on
the drums. Today he has gone all whiny just because
I took my saucepans off him for going dink donk
on them with his hammer and lectric drill.

Smells said I must give him loads of gold for buying him a pop star suit plus proper drums. But I said, "Gold, what gold? Who was the 1 that blew up my safe with gunpowder so my gold went chinkle plonk all over Frettnin Forest? It was YOU!"

Now he is out in the Forest having a look and a wander with his metal detector, saying he will be rich soonly, so nah nah.

Can you take him back to the Lair with you, please pleeeeze PLEEEEEEEEZ? You know you miss him, yesss?

Yours hopingly,

Little Wolf

Dear Mum and Dad,

Your note sounds a small bit grrrrrish about me letting Smells have a wander by himself. I do not know Y, he comes indoors when he is starving (eg a lot). Beeeeesides, you always say give in to him, it is the only way.

Also you say you are not having him back just at the mo, but let you know if he has any luck with his metal detector, then you might have another think.

9

Now I will say my news. We are a bit short of snacks here (not much rabbits in Frettnin Forest any more, boo shame). Yeller (best friend and cuz) is not staying with me in my house. He has gone off southly for a rabbit hunt and private Lone Wolf  practiss. I miss his cheery shouting. It is very quiet, except for Smells whining.

Normus Bear has gone away huntingly 2, only not southly. He is more westly so he can tickle trouts (not rabbits) out of Spring River down the

valley by Lonesome Woods, Murkshire. Plus looking privately for a nice hibernaty cave for snoozing in when the snow comes. I miss his rufftuff ways.

Stubbs has knitted himself a nice twiggy nest on the roof. He thinks he can fly better if he starts from high up.

I can hear him going "Ark" to the big crows sometimes, but I do not see him a lot like I used to, only when he has a small *ark*sident and falls down the chimney hole.

Mum, any rabbit rolls going spare, yes?

Yours hintingly,

Petit Starver (French)

The Big Old Place that Used to **Belong to Uncle Bigbad,** FRETTNIN FOREST, BEASTSHIRE

Down the garden

Dear Mum and Dad,

I got a postcard from Normus today saying wish you were hairy (joke). He says he is having a nice time only a bit 2 much trout maybe, also no luck with caves.

You say you have got new ~~naybores~~, ~~nayboors~~, people next door called Fang and Mauler Snarl-Wolfington – they sound posh, but are they nice noisy wuns?

Yours interestedly,

L Wolf

12

The Lav

Dear Mum and Dad,

Yeller says Arrrrrooooo by a short note to let me know he has made himself cosy in a nice smelly hole, not 2 sunny in the morningtime. It is a good place for having new ideas about funny tricks ect.

Here is a good 1 he sent me for tricking your mum. Go into the lav, get some toilet paper, go round and round with it till you are covered up, then shout, "Mummy Mummy."

If your mummy comes along wurrid, saying, "Yes?", then you say (hollow voice) "So am I, har har!"

13

Here is my Cheesy Toothpaste trick I sent him back. Get sum Skweezy Cheesy in a tube, cross out the words on it saying Skweezy Cheesy and put Toothpaste. Then if your dad says, "Hoy pack in cleaning your teeth all the time!" you say, "Har Har, I am eating cheese really."

Yours chucklingly,

Little

PS For this toothpaste trick you can use any old tube of food like condensation milk, but not glue, Ok? (Bit harsh).

Dear Mum and Dad,

Thank you for your gruff letter saying pack in tricking and start hunting for a ~~nowrushing~~ ~~newrishing~~ ~~murishing~~ joosy snack for your poor little sweetypaws, Smells. You do not menshun my tummy what has gone small as a small ant. Never mind, off I go suddenly to fetch Smells a nice fat moosy or a buffalo, maybe. So do not blame me if he gets the windy bumps like normal for not chewing proply.

Yours,

A Noid

Dear Mum and Dad,

Thank you for the nice pic of the posh new people next door that Dad took with his new spy-camera strapped to his knee.

Shame he did not tuck the camera up higher in his hearole, I like pics with faces on. Never mind.

You say their lair has 5 sleepholes and 2 lickrooms, plus they have a really really really clever cub called Spoiler who knows THE LOT.

Plus you say he is a proper brute beast, not a small weaky like me that only likes reading and writing.

Now I am all upset.

Yours jealously,

Littly

PS Do not tell Spoiler any of our tricks, case he steals them, Ok?

PPS Smells has just come in all wet but still no gold.

PPPS Yes I am going to give him some grub NOW. It is my hedgehog. I was saving as a treat 4 me, but never mind.

Dear errr umm, is that Mud and Dam or are you my Mim and Dood?

Yesterday I played cleaning out my earwax with gunpowder, so my brane went off bang, shame, eh?

Now I bet you will say, "Oh shock, our best eldest cub, no more fine letters from him, he has gone and got ~~hamknees~~ ~~armniece~~ ~~amsneezia~~ lost his memory! Now he will forget we are fierce wolves and think we are just fat peabugs with fur coats on, oo-er, sob sob ect."

True, plus I cannot remember the name of my baby bruv even, so no chance I can look after him for you any more, sorry. Now he will have to come back to the Lair and chew your videos for a change.

Yours trickingly,

Thingy

PS Good 1, yes? Did you get it? It was me really.

PPS Dad's spy pics are getting better, yes? Spoiler is very hansum, eh? (fib fib).

My real address (not a trick wun, honest)

The Big Old Place that Used to **Belong to Uncle Bigbad,** FRETTNIN FOREST, BEASTSHIRE

Dear Mum and Dad,

Not fair you sending Smellybreff that parcel with the spanking machine in, just because of 1 small trick letter from me. Also the machine was batteries not included. So Smells has pinched all my wuns out of my torch, my Walkwolf, and my swimmy bathfrog ect. Just so the machine would chase me round going **s w i s h bonk o w**.

Also, thanks for your crool postcard that you sent saying serve you right plus instruckshuns. All right I will look after Smells for ages more, but tell him to pack in being a fusspot, saying he only likes eating Krispy Ducklets with Moosepops, also skweezing brown sauce in the keyholes, not funny.

I did not mean to say you *were* fat peabugs. That was a short joke, only I forgot about Dad being a lergic to fun.

Yours warmbottly,

L Wolf

PS I hope those batteries pack up soon,

Dear Mum and Dad,

Thank you for your moany reply, very newsy but damp. (Smells dropped it down the lav, so cubbish.) It was kwite hard reading it with lots of the ink gone spready.

You say you are absolutely dis-something (is it custard?) because of the Snarl-Wolfingtons being so posh and rich and us only poorish now.

Also you say you are fed up about them always boasting about their son Spoiler. He is getting faymuss by being Pack Leader of his own fearsum wolfpack and him only 3 times my age and bigness.

Y is he always getting his pic in *Wolf Weekly*
for facing something I cannot read? Is it clanger
or dancer? No wait, it might be DANGER he
keeps facing, oh I get it.

You say what about me? "Have you done
anything for us to have a good boast about?"
Answer YES, I am
giving Uncle
Bigbad's big old
house a fine sortout!
Plus I am being a
good cub-sitter for
Smells and letting
him eat all my
snowy weather
snacks.

More tomorrowly,

Busyboy

Dear Mum and Dad,

Before, I was feeling a bit downinthedumper
so I thought, blow it, best thing if you are
onyourownly is think of a new fun thing to do.

So phew, yesterday I got all Uncle Bigbad's bits
and pieces together that he had in this big old
~~manshun~~ ~~mantyion~~
house before he died of
the jumping beanbangs!
(All the beds out the
dorm, the desks, the
blackboards ect.)
I put them all in 1 lot
of rooms upstairs. Then
I did a posh notice on
the door saying,
L Wolf's
Interesting Museum.

24

Today I am making a place for all the
adventure stuff that me and Yeller had when we
turned Cunning College into Adventure Academy.
(I had 1 quick go on the zipwire, just 4 luck.)

WHEEE-

BONK!)

Next I will make a place in the cellar for all our Haunted Hall bits we had when we were teaching small brutes haunty tricks, wooooo.

Then after, I will make 1 more place for all our Forest Detective Agency fingerprint kits, magnifying glasses, ect.

Guess what I will be then? A museum keeper! Loads of brute beasts will love to have a rummage in Uncle Bigbad's old house, plus have a laugh with his small naughty nephew, I bet!

Yours rushaboutly,

Little

Dear Mum and Dad,

You say museums are rubbish, also pack in that sissy tidying, it is no good for boasting about. But I am not tidying, I told you, I am having a sortout.

You say it is still all my fault that Mr and Mrs Snarl-Wolfington keep swanking about their son Spoiler. And now he has a Mobilair all of his ownly. You say Y cannot I be all mature like him? I 'spect you are jealous, just because of him buying it out of his own pocket money that his Gran gave him for being **a credit to his long family name**. Not fair, blaming me if he keeps driving

27

splashingly through puddles near you saying,
"Good wun, yah?"

Anyhow, I have not got a pocket to put
Granny money in. Plus, you know I have not
even got a Granny, not since she got her temper
up and ate herself.

Yours chindownly,

Little

PS What is RHYWP?

Dear Mum and Dad,

Thank you for your crool news about some lucky wolves having oldest cubs to be proud of. True I have not got a Mobilair or a pack of my own. BUT (big but) I am giving in to Smells, plus I am better at reading and joined-up writing than their oldest cub, I bet.

Also, you say that RHYWP stands for REALLY HARSH YOUNG WOLF PACK and that Spoiler is getting ready to drive his Mobilair to Frettnin Forest and camp!

29

What a big cheek he has got! Frettnin Forest
has got enuff proud wolves, called me and Smells.
So if he comes parking himself, I will have a
good spy of his harsh habits, then I will see him
off, no messing. I will say (rumbly voice), "Hoy
you, buzz off out of our forest, OK yah?" Then
he will think, "Oh no, sorry, we are trespassing on
Little Wolf's land, he sounds posh and tuff,
Cheero."

Yours shockingly,

L Wolf (Gold Badness Badge)

Dear Mum and Dad,

You know I put up that notice on my front door saying Interesting Museum ect the other day? Well, guess what? *Today* I had a visitor. She was a little old lady in a bonnet and she had gingery whiskers plus a peppery smell. Also she was interested in seeing if there was a big safe with gold in it from the days when Uncle Bigbad had Cunning College. Then she looked into my eyes and I felt a bit swimmy in the head, then off she went swiftly so I did not see her any more, boo shame.

Plus remember I said about not many rabbits? Now I have found out Y. It is Mister Twister the Fox and Master of Dizgizzes (still cannot spell it). He has been capturing loads of them with a crafty poster stuck by nail to many a tree in Frettnin Forest. I am sending you 1.

Yours,  ly,

Little Wolf

PS Clever trick, eh? But whyo Y does he want to pinch them all? There are loads 2 many for 1 crafty fox to eat!

ATTENTION ALL YOU TUBBY BUNNIES

Feeling a bit too plump and succulent?
Need to shed a few juicy pounds but can't afford
pricey gym-fees?
Then just wave it all goodbye with Sackracer™
With Sackracer™ it's simple!

- Pop into the sack

- Hop over Windy Ridge to the Dark Hills

- Look out for a rabbit hole with 'free carrots' sign

- Pause for a delicious, healthy snack

You'll be amazed how tasty you can look with
very little effort.
Send now for your free trial Sackracer™ to
TWISTER CORPORATION, THE DEN,
BROKEN TOOTH CAVES, DARK HILLS, BEASTSHIRE

The Big Old Place that Used to Belong to Uncle Bigbad,

FRETTNIN FOREST, BEASTSHIRE

Dear Mum and Dad,

Thank you for the nice fearsum pic of Dad
saying, "Pack in that museum or else." Plus
the extra GRRRRS you sent for me saying
Yours 🖐 ly about Mister Twister. Now I
am all puffed out by repeating, "I must not be
impressed by foxy tricks, they are rubbish,"
1 millium times. Plus, you say I must HURRY
UP and think of good ways
to capture Mister Twister
quick, just because he is
a big Foe to us
wolves. Also, so I can
claim the huge reward
and send it to you,
yes? Then you can be
rich like the Snarl–
Wolfingtons plus having a
Number 1 son to boast about.

I have had a good study of that Reward poster you sent of Mister Twister ~~in his latest dis-skies dussgize~~ dressed up. I will try my tuffest to capture him, but it will be a hard job I bet because of so many trees round here just like him.

Yours keenly,

L B Wolf

WANTED BY MURKSHIRE POLICE

MISTER TWISTER
THE FOX
ARCH CROOK,
MASTER OF DISGUISE
AND HYPNOTIST

The public are advised not to look into his eyes or let him talk softly to them.

HUGE REWARD FOR CAPTURE!

The Dorm

Dear Mum and Dad,

Guess what woke me up this morning? A loud Blah Blah coming south-eastly to my ears.

It came from a loudshouter saying, "Spoiler calling, Pack Leader of The Really Harsh Young Wolf Pack, OK yah? Now pay attention all you weaky wolves round here, and that means YOU, Little Wolf. You have been far too soft, letting

Mr Twister get away with his criminal behaviour for so long, yah? All right, listen up! I and my RHYWP intend to put that fox in a box pretty darn sharpish, right?

So if you want to be part of the action, trot yourselves over to my Mobilair on the north shore of Lake Lemming and get some proper training. I am prepared to train you in Harshness, Tracking, Being More Crafty than Foxes, and Capturing. If you obey orders and accept me as your Pack Leader, I might even let you have a little tiddly bit of the HUGE REWARD I intend to earn from turning Mr Twister over to the police. Now get a shift on! Because if you don't come to us at the double, we will come and fetch you! No matter how deep you dig, we'll come and pull you out of your hidy-hole by your teeny tiny tail, I kid you not, yah? Roger and Out."

You know Uncle Bigbad used to say, "Blinking Blunker?" Well I think Spoiler is 1. He made all my neckhairs get stiffed up. Out of bed I jumped rushingly to give him a sharp seeing off! Only I could not go straight over because I had to wait for Smells to put on his engine driver outfit plus oily rag. Not fair, just because his small brane thinks training goes woo woo chuff chuff.

Never mind, ready now, off we go!

Yours sternly,

L Bad Wolf,
Son of Gripper

Dear Mum and Dad,

Now I will say my news about Smells and me
arriving at Lake Lemming shore. He was sad
because of no trains but he got more cheery
because I let him put a rubber duck on his head
and go in the reeds to do spying with me
crawlingly.

1st we met some coots (they
were kwite tasty). Then on the shore
we spied Spoiler doing camping with his Really
Harsh Young Wolf Pack. Spoiler has got many a
big snarler in his pack. They are big huge cubs,
more like dadsize really. I like the uniform they
wear, it is tracksuity (shadow colour), plus big
writing on the back saying RHYWP.

You can tell Spoiler, he is the biggest 1 with the dark glasses on plus a SPOILER, PACK LEADER T-shirt.

His best saying is, "Listen up, guys!" in a posh way for bossing about. He makes his pack call him PL. Like, if they hear him say an order, they have to say back, "OK yah, PL, sound idea!" They all like jogging bunchedupply along by the shore, singing ambush songs.

Yours spyingly,

Quack (code name)

PS We are going posting this and then have another spy after.

Dear Mum and Dad,

Today we got ambushed, all because of Smells being a hopeless spy.

Spoiler's pack came over to the lake for a poke about in the reeds. I said whisperingly, "Quick, Smells, make some duck noises," and he went "**woof woof moo moo**," so selfish.

Did I say about the lectric fence, no? Well I am inside it. Also I am in a small secret cell, but not sure what happened to Smells except I can hear him saying, "yah yah yah" all the time.

Yours lockedinly,

LW

Dear Mum and Dad,

Now I will say about the inside of the Mobilair. It has got a driving part in the front plus all cosy up the back, a bit like normal lairs but more modern with loads of lectric things going hmmm. For example, a fridge full of Moosejoose in the kitchen (yum, yes please). There is a lav and lickroom, plus proper dark smelly corners for curlups. Plus it has got this cell I am kept in behind a secret panel and only Spoiler knows the combination to open it. The outside of the

Mobilair is all armour-plated with a lectric fence going round outside, so hard to have a sneaky peep in.

Spoiler gave me a hard Chinese burn saying, "Go on, give in, say 'You are my Pack Leader and I want to join the RHYWP and be trained by you!'" But I said, "No way, never never ect." Plus I was not trembly at all, hardly.

Yours stubbornly,

L Wolf

PS Ooo-ow my arm.

Dear Mum and Dad,

Today, Spoiler did **Get Your Mussels Up**
with his pack by chewing rocks, pressups,
running ect.

Also he made the RHYWP do Harshness tests
like Jump in the Lake till you go Blue, plus
Backbiting, Ripping, Insulting, ect.

Not fair. Grinder, Biff, Grey and Sleek keep saying I am a small sissy, plus I am 2 humble to be in their pack anyway. Also, I heard Grabber tell Smoke that I did not come out of the Top Drawer or go to a Top School so sucks to me. So I said, "Maybe not but here is a Top Insult. You come out of my Top Drawer, you are pants har har!" But they did not laugh, so moody.

They keep making a big fuss of Smells, going pat pat tickle tickle, but not right now with the sun falling in the water. Right now they are all looking at a big map mumblingly, saying, "Mister Twister, Mister Twister, abslootly, deffnly, we'll get the blighter, BIG money reward, OK no sweat, yah?"

Yours listeningly,

A Left (new code name)

Dear Mum and Dad,

Guess what? I am freeeeeeeee, Spoiler uncaptured me! First he made me listen to his pack howling Ambush Songs till after the bong of midnight. The words are rubbish but I will put 1 down for you in posh writing anyhow.

Spoiler is our Leader yeah!
We are harsh and we don't care!
Our Wolf Pack is Number 1!
We know how to spoil your fun!

We like taking it in turns,
To give weakies Chinese burns.
Listen up and listen good!
We can bite through lumps of wood.

Really Harsh Young Wolves are we,
The Hairy Scary WP!
This is tuff but this is true
We have ways to capture you!

Mister Twister, you're no good,
You are just a milky pud!
Mister Twister can't you see,
You can't hide from the WP!

PUSH! PUSH! AMBUSH!

But all I kept saying bravely was, "You cannot scare me in my own forest. You are just big snobs and bullies! I am L Wolf, Son of Gripper, Nephew of Bigbad, grrrr ect."

So in the end Spoiler came tapping in the combination that undid the lock of my secret cell. He let me out, saying, "Oh go away, you teeny fluffball, we are not wasting our time training you. Trot along and don't come back till you've grown some fur on your chest, right? I've got *important* brute beasts to capture, like Mister Twister for a start, so it's time for me to take a little looksee.

Hey, and remember, your baby brother is with me now. So don't try any of your tricks to stop me earning my huge reward, OK yah? Or Smellybreff might get upset in a BIG way, you follow?"

Grinder, Biff, Grey and Sleek gave me a Chinese burn each for luck. Then the RHYWP packed up the lectric fence, jumped in the Mobilair and off they drove quick with headlights on.

Yours sorewristly,

L Wolf

PS I forgot to say about Smells. Spoiler has let him tie himself to the radiator of his Mobilair, so he can be a mascot. Now he will have a thrill and let Spoiler be his Pack Leader - so shaming for his big brother.

Dear Mum and Dad,

2 much awakeness last night, now I am soooo tired and upset.

It is not because of so much Chinese burns, but I did not like them laughing plus calling me small fluffball. I chased after the Mobilair but my legs do not go round as fast as wheels, so no good. Then I sat pantingly in the blackness saying to me (big breff), "Listen, you are all on your ownly, your friends are faraway, your baby bruv has gone off with harsh strangers. Plus you are in the middle of a dark damp forest, nothing 2 eat, no torch. Now have a think. What would Mum and Dad do now?"

Answer, # HOWL!

So I did. Quick as a chick I ran and ran through Frettnin Forest, in and out of the deep shadows howling, "HELP! HELP!" and "WHERE ARE YOU, SMELLS?" Sad to say I was just going round and round, banging into trees.

Also tripping over roots with my puff hot in my throat, seeing fat monsters and slimy spooks everywhere. Then I got giddy, so I fell over and bonked my head.

Your sorry boy,

Littly

Dear Mum and Dad,

Guess who found me and stitched a nice quilt of dry leaves with his clever beak for warmness? Stubbs! All because of a small crowd of rooks I woke up in the night-time with my howling. They flew south past Stubby's nest on the roof of my house the next day and said to him rookly about me going Help Bonk.

So Stubbs said "Ark!" meaning *Ark*shun Stations, and did his best flying, looking 4 me. But when he did not see fluff nor fur of me, back he flew to Frettnin Forest. Good thing, because he found me up the top edge of it, curled up dead nearly.

I said, "I am so shamed, Stubbs, I have let down the name of wolf by losing Smells to the RHYWP." But he said, "Ark!" meaning Open your be*ark*. Then he gave me a good snack of chewy wigglers he found eating a treestump. So now I am all strong again. I am going to sit him on my head most of the way home (saves wings) but he can flap up above the trees now and then for a look, in case of me going the wrong way.

Yours homewardly,

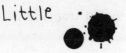

Home, you know

The Big Old Place that Used to **Belong to Uncle Bigbad,** FRETTNIN FOREST, BEASTSHIRE

Dear Mum and Dad,

Me and Stubbs had another chat today, me all cosy in bed, him on the picture rail. It was *ark*cellent. I told him all about Spoiler and his Mobilair and how he has got Smells as his mascot (so shaming for his big brother). Stubbs said, "Ark! Ark!" meaning *Ark*tually, he saw some wheely tr*ark*s when he was looking for me flying flappingly, 1st eastly over the River Riggly as far as Hazardous Canyon.

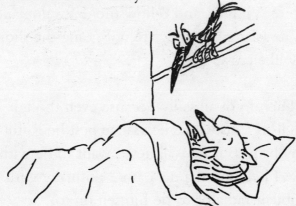

But the tr*ark*s were not going into the Canyon, they were going northly maybe towards Pointy Peaks on the border between Beastshire and Grimshire.

Maybe the RHYWP are going towards the White Wildness and Yellowsmoke Swamplands, or to Vile Island, but they are not going the short way like crows fly!

Then I got all sadly because even though Smells is a ~~noosance~~ ~~newsance~~ pest he is still my baby bruv. But he will never want to be with me now, I bet, boo shame. I am 2 unthrilly with no Mobilair radiator to tie himself on to.

Stubbs said, "Ark!" meaning B*ark* yourself up!
That is enuff Sorry for Yourselfness!

I said, "Yes but not
fair being just 1 small
wolf v. Spoiler plus all
his harsh RHYWPs!"

 Stubbs said back, "Ark" times
3! meaning I hope you are
being *sark*astic, because what
about Stubby Crow,
*Ark*sqwire, plus your 2 other
rem*ark*able chums?"

I said, "Do you think Yeller and Normus
would give up their private time just to come
and help me?" Stubbs answered, "Ark!" meaning
Ark you kidding? Course they would!

Your hopeful boy,

Little

Dear Mum and Dad,

Off went Stubbs today after double worms for his br*ark*fast. I gave him a good launch off the roof with our new Crowspeeder we made spesh.

If his wings are good flappers, maybe he can deliver 2 arkmails in 1 single day, saying,

Emerjuncy shock. Come back to my house quick, I need your help! A strange pack of posh wolves has turned Smells's head. I must go and get him back by hick or by trick. Sorry for ~~inconveen~~ inconveinyunce mucking you about,

Your friendly, LBW.

Then I got out my detective stuff from the museum. See, it was good having that tidyup! Plus my rucksack, maps, tent, ect for a dustoff. Also Smells's ted, in case he wants to be my baby bruv again. I shall practiss my hicks and tricks and tracking, for I must be off soonly and find Spoiler. He needs showing who is Top Wolf of Beastshire, huff puff!

Yours Big Badly,

Little

The Big Old Place that Used to Belong to Uncle Bigbad, FRETTNIN FOREST, BEASTSHIRE

Dear Mum and Dad,

Arrrooo!!! Normus has come already with loads of trouts for snacks. Nice, but they give you a coff from all the hairy bones. When I opened the door 4 him, he gave me a hard bearhug saying, "Good to see you, Littly. Trout tickling is fun but not good fun like bashing. Don't you get wurrid! Where is that posh wolfpack of strangers? Let me go and give them a hard punch up the bunch of them!"

I said I did not know xactly where they went but they were looking for Mister Twister out eastly. Normus said, "Fancy those Harshies turning Smells's head round! That is so crool! He is only a small teddycub!"

You know I said in my arkmails the RHYWP has turned Smells's head? Well Normus does not understand sayings. He thinks they really have turned Smells's head round the other way. Never mind, it is nice he wants to help keenly, eh? But where is Yeller and where is Stubbs? Oo-er, I hope Spoiler has not caught them by trick or trap.

Yours ankshussly,

Little

Dear Mum and Dad,

My best news is about Yeller. He has come at last. Bit slow, but not his fault and no tricking or trapping by Spoiler, arrrooooo! Stubbs was so weak from his arkstra long fly, 1st westly then southly, Yeller had to do 1st aid on him by popping him down his vest for a warmup. Plus feed him mushy peabugs by eyedropper.

Yeller said, "HELLO LICKLE! HOW'S TRICKS?" Then he gave me a funny pawshake with his arm going, "Tootle-toot!"  (Not really, it was a false skweezy 1, he had it on for a joke!) Then we had loads of rabbit rolls he brought from down south, yes please, yum yum. Plus saving all the chewy bits for Stubbs to get his strongness up. Yeller said loudly how he liked being private for short times, spesh if there are rabbits handy. But more fun is helping your chums find the RHYWP and Mr Twister. Plus thinking of Big Ideas and tricks for fixing problems together. We are all 2 tiredout for talking now, but we will know what to do by tomorrow, I bet, by having a good pow-wow.

Yours feelingbetterly,

 Little

Dear Mum and Dad,

Do not fret and frown, we will soon have Smells back. Probly.

I told the chums about Spoiler, how he thinks he is Top Wolf not just in Murkshire where my Mum and Dad live (that is you, just in case you are not sure, OK?) but even here in Beastshire. Also I xplained about the bigness of his harsh wolfpack, plus his Mobilair going a lot quicker than wolf cubs. Then I told them about getting captured, plus Smells going away with the RHYWP to be their mascot.

Quick as a chick they all wanted to go and fight Spoiler. Yeller said loudly, "POOR OLD LICKLE, SO SHAMIN FOR YOUR PROUD NAME OF WOLF! LET ME HELP YOU. Y DON'T WE RUSH AFTER THEM AND DO A SHOCKIN TRICK ON SPOILER?"

I said, "Thank you, most kind. Plus we must capture Mister Twister before Spoiler does, so we can get the huge reward."

Yeller said, "NO NEED TO GET WURRID ABOUT SPOILER GETTIN THERE FIRST, LICKLE! NOBODY KNOWS WHERE MISTER TWISTER LIVES. HOY! WAIT A MO! I KNOW WHERE THERE MIGHT BE A GOOD CLUE! LET'S GO AND HAVE ANOTHER LOOK AT HIS TRICK POSTER FOR GETTIN RABBICKS TO JUMP INTO SACKS!"

So off we went pantingly to a tree with the bunny poster on. And yes, it says on the poster about hop along to Windy Ridge! Also it has got an address in Broken Tooth Caves on the bott! Arrrrooo for Yeller!

Your cheery boy,

Little

Dear Mum and Dad,

You know I did that cheery arrrroooo in my last note? Sorry, that came out a bit 2 quick. Because Normus, Yeller and Stubbs keep forgetting 1 thing. I said, "I know my name Wolf is just a short 1, not like Snarl-Wolfington, but I must not let Spoiler keep doing more daring deeds than me, or I will let it right down. It is me must get Smells back, plus capture Mr Twister, not you."

Then Normus said buttinly, "Oh no, Little, this job is much too big for 1 small wolfcub. You say Spoiler and the RHYWP are gnashing for a bashing. They are big and harsh, so bashing

them is the only way, with harder biting and Chinese burns. They have all got miles bigger

mussels than you. I will go and do the bashing,
you know I like it."

I said, "No, Normus. I have to be a lone wolf
and do it all on my ownly, or Mum
and Dad will say: Nar Nar bubbacub, you are
just a blubbercub!"

Then Stubbs said, "Ark!" meaning Stop *ark*uing.
I will fly high up and drop crowstuff on Spoiler's
head, plus his RHYWP. Yeller said, "WHAT
SORT OF STUFF, STUBBY?" Stubbs said,
"Ark!" meaning I'll whisp*ark*. Then Yeller said,
"OH, I SEE, THAT SORT OF STUFF. YEAH,
WELL, THAT WOULD BE
GOOD, BUT BETTER IF
YOU COULD TEACH
A BIG HERD OF
ELEPHANTS FLYIN,
HAR HAR!"

It is nice to have a laugh, even if you are
feeling more low than a worm's tummy button.

Yours notsureyettly,

Little

The Big Old Place that Used to **Belong to Uncle Bigbad,** FRETTNIN FOREST, BEASTSHIRE

Special thinky spot, under chair by my desk

Dear Mum and Dad,

Something proud happened to me today, here it is.

Our pow-wows have been looooooooooooong wuns with many a 'Trouble is' in them.

I will say Yeller's latest loud 'Trouble is' for you. He said, "TROUBLE IS, HAVIN THE RHYWP MEANS THAT SPOILER HAS GOT EYES AND EARS EVERYWHERE. HE HAS GOT MANY A WET NOSE TO SNIFF WITH, PLUS LOADS OF LEGS TO RUN WITH, PLUS HUNDREDS OF TEETH TO BITE WITH. NO LONE BRUTE CAN DEFEAT HIM, LICKLE. ONLY A WOPPIN BIG STRONG WOLFPACK WILL DO IT – AND WHERE WILL WE FIND WUN IN ALL THIS LAND?"

I was all upset, BUT (big but), just then, a fine thought jumped in my head. Ding! I said, "Maybe we cannot find a ***wopping big strong*** wolfpack! But I think I know where to find a ***Spesh*** sort of pack, with only a few brute beasts in maybe, but brave and keen!"

All the chums jumped up saying, "Where, where, where?"

And I said answeringly, "Right here, because that Spesh pack is US!"

Your braney boy,

Me (Clue: not any of the others)

Dear Mum and Dad,

Here is my new news about that Spesh sort of pack I said about. Normus was a bit wurrid saying, "But Little, what about bear cubs? Packs are only for wolves, aren't they?"

I said, "Not our Spesh pack, Normus, you can be in ours!" So he said OK, he wanted to join and do some dyb-dob-dybbing.

Still, Stubbs was not sure, saying, "Ark!" meaning *ark*scuse me, how can crowchicks be in packs?

I said, "Easy cheesy, you just say you want to be IN!" So he said, "Ark!" meaning *Ark*-kay, he wanted to.

Yeller shouted, "COR, I LIKE THIS IDEA, I'M JOININ 2 AND I HAVE THOUGHT UP A GOOD NAME FOR OUR PACK. WE CAN BE CALLED SPOBB, SHORT FOR **S**MALL **P**ACK **O**F **B**RUTE **B**EASTS."

Then Normus said hopingly, "Are we going to be Harsh like the RHYWP?"

I said, "Us SPOBBs are not copycubs! No, we are just going to capture Mister Twister, rescue Smells off Spoiler plus have a load of fun!"

So now our full short name is SPOBBTHALOF (**S**mall **P**ack **o**f **B**rute **B**easts **t**hat **H**ave **a** **L**oad **o**f **F**un). We did three loud Arrrrooooos for it and quick as a chick, Stubbs made us all SPOBBTHALOF badges with his clever beak.

Plus, guess what? He did me a posh T-shirt saying LITTLE WOLF, PACK LEADER on the chesty side!

Yours proudly,

Little Wolf, (PL)

PS Yeller wants us to do some short SPOBBTHALOF PAWBOOKS so I will send you 1 soonly, yes?

SPOBBTHALOF

Dear Mum and Dad,

Not much time to write because of Packtraining, but here is a bit of our Pawbook. Yeller did the writing, so it is fine and shouty, also quite hilly.

THE SPOBBTHALOF PAW AND CLAW BOOK

how you join   JUST SAY HEY! YOU KNOW ME.
IN IS WHERE I WANT TO BE!

members
- LICKLE WOLF, PL (GOT WISSUL) - TENTER, TRACKER
- YELLER WOLF (BEST FRIEND AND CUZ) - TOP TRICKER AND COOKER
- NORMUS BEAR - BASHER AND SWIMMER
- STUBBY CROW - HI-SPYER NOTTER AND BADGEMAKER
- PLUS SMELLS (BUT ONLY IF HE STOPS BEIN A SPOILER MASCOT)

71

motto BE SPESH

rules
- 👣 do not have 2 many rules (2 strikt)
- 🐾 have a load of fun
- 👣 stick up for our motto
- 🐾 have campin in tents, also in dens, bivvies and that
- 👣 NO MOBILAIRS
- 🐾 make things
- 👣 no doing chinese burns on each other
- 🐾 better tricks than sticks (but Normus gets first bash in emerjuncy)

watch this space

just in case,
of short new rule
(not sad but cool)

Did you like the 'Claw' part of our Paw and Claw Book? Yeller put that in for Stubbs spesh, because of crows not having normal paws.

Yours proudly,

Little Wolf, Pack Leader

Dear Mum and Dad,

I am sitting on a comfy molehill not far from Windy Ridge. And guess what? Our flag is UP, arrrrrrroooooo! Our 4-brute Pack Tent will be up soonly 2, I bet.

SPOBBTHALOF

But we did not go unplanningly from my house, oh no. 1st we did rucksack packing. It was so hard because of tent poles, matches, bedrolls, tweezers, torches, pencils, frying pans, snacks, alphabetti spaghetti plus tins of bakebeans (canteen size), I love them kiss kiss!

Also knife, fork, spoon, nets, glue, toggles, woggles, foggles, joggles, sleepybags, string plus noodly pots, notebooks, plasters, kebab sticks, ect.

Normus's pack was a bit 2 big but then Stubbs made him take out the sofa, so a bit better.

Then off we went quickmarchingly through Frettnin Forest, going leftright leftright, searchy search for Smells ect.

Where we are going is a secret so I will write it smally. Broken Tooth Caves, shhhh.

Yours blownaboutly,

Little

PS I forgot to say Y we are going to you know where. No time now. Maybe tomorrow, yes?

Dear Mum and Dad,

Brrrr, blowy up here, plus dark as dark. Also, it is hard to sleep so I am writing tiredoutly by torch going flash.

Look, I have done you some pics of us doing tents. That is me with the wissul.

This is our 1st go, it was rubbish, because only a small shower curtain really.

This is our next go (Stubbs made it with his clever beak out of table cloth). Yes, it is a bit squashy, also Normus will not all go in.

Last night we did our 1st sleep-in-1-tent-practiss. The practiss was good but not the sleep. Stubbs says never mind, he can knit a nice bivvy out of twigs for us (bit like a nest only other way upply) so maybe more snoozy. Also, 1 other good thing, I thought up some tent rules to go in the space in our Paw and Claw Books.

Tent Rules

🐾 Normus, be careful, no rolling over on people, Ok?

🐾 No bundling

🐾 No itchy food

🐾 No lickwashing after the bong of midnight

🐾 Go to the lav before zipflaps time (but not in the tent, yes?)

It's sunjumpup time now, so we are hunting small wigglers for breakfast. Then packing, then tracking!

Yours yawningly,

Laaaaaahtle (with a yawn in, get it?)

Dear Mum and Dad,

Up and down we go marchingly today, over the Dark Hills. Look out Broken Tooth Caves (sssshhh, remember), here comes the SPOBBTHALOFs! Oh yes, I was going to say before, Y we decided to go there. Ready? Here is Y.

We had a short campfire practiss before we went off packly. We had alphabetti spaghetti, hmmm nice! I did some writing in it like this.

Then round the campfire we played Branestorm, so our branes could have a strong think of sum ideas. I put them all down in my notebook like this:

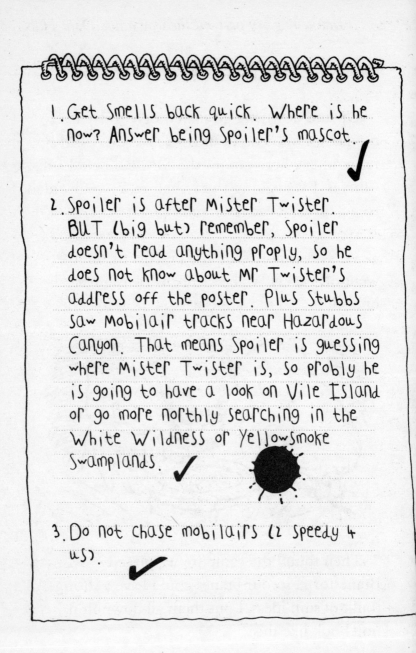

1. Get smells back quick. Where is he now? Answer being Spoiler's mascot. ✔

2. Spoiler is after Mister Twister. BUT (big but) remember, Spoiler doesn't read anything proply, so he does not know about Mr Twister's address off the poster. Plus Stubbs saw mobilair tracks near Hazardous Canyon. That means Spoiler is guessing where Mister Twister is, so probly he is going to have a look on Vile Island or go more northly searching in the White Wildness or Yellowsmoke Swamplands. ✔

3. Do not chase mobilairs (2 speedy 4 us). ✔

4. Best to find Mister Twister and wait by him till Spoiler comes his way. ✓

5. Where is Mister Twister? Answer, not sure xactly. Oh yes, his address says 'The Den, Broken Tooth Caves', but he is soooo crafty, maybe that is just a trick to trick packs! Never mind, we will go and look for clues there anyway. ✓

6. Hard part. Capture Mister Twister, then send out a message saying "Nar Nar Spoiler, what are you going to do about it?" (Normus's idea) ✓

7. Very hard part. When Spoiler comes, SPOBBS do an ambush on him and his RHYWP then uncapture smells.

The End

Must go now to do secret tracking ~~sing sine~~
sign practiss, just in case of somewun getting lost,
ect.

For xample,

That means 'Smells went that way', get it?

Yours leadingly,

LW (PL)

Dear Mum and Dad,

I will say to you by tracking sign what we are doing.

Now, if you did not say, "Aha, that means Spread Out Everybody," then go in the corner with a pointy hat on saying Duncehead (only kidding, not really Dad).

I said to my pack, "Let us do Spreadouting just so we can go all round Mister Twister, then close in tight on him all of a suddenly. It will be like sharp teeth on a mice pie, what do you think SPOBBs?" Then they said, "Cor, fine Pack Leading, Little!" so I am feeling all proud.

Stubbs is Spreadouting eastly for a good look over Vile Island, ect. Yeller and Normus are Spreadouting 2 different ways over the Dark Hills. So guess where I am off 2? I am going straight up northly, across the Parching Plain, to see if I can spot fur or fluff of Mister Twister up near Borderlands Market.

Yours offwetrottly,

L Wolf

Dear Mum and Dad,

I am in Parching Plain, it is hot as hot but not 1 pool or stream to wet my tongue in. Also you get sharp thorns and stones in your pads, plus 2 claws bust, boo shame.

The best thing is the wind going woooooo but not the dust, it gets up your smellholes. Not many big hungry birds have come flicking me with their shadows.

Good thing because I forgot to bring Yeller's kite, the 1 with eyes painted on it, so no going flip and flap in their ugly face. Never mind, I have got out my tentpole. Now if they try making a snack out of me, I will give them a shocking poke with the pointy end.

Sometimes you see some scaly crawlers going wiggle, but no large brute beasts yet. BUT (big but) I have found some dinosaur tracks like this.

I am having a wonder, is it that crafty fox in a clever dizgizze? (Cannot spell it.) Off I go.

Yours warmly,

The Panter

Dear Mum and Dad,

You know that dinosaur?
It was not Mister Twister, plus
it was not a dinosaur. It was a
nostrich! He is funny, no fur
at all. He is like a grate big
feathery ball, plus tall bare
legs with just skin on, plus his
neck is like the hose off my
vacuum cleaner!

I said, "Hello, I am Little Wolf, have you seen a
crafty fox called Mister Twister by any chance?"
Then guess what? He went "oo-er" all of a
suddenly and stuck his head down a hole.

I said, "Sorry to interrupt, are you looking for a snack?" Then his tall legs went all twitchy and I thought, "Look out, he might give me a hard kick!" But no, he just said back (muffly voice), "Thank you. Call again, Mister Wolf, I am not at home today."

I said replyingly, "Good joke! But do not fret and fear, I want a nice ride not a nostrich stew. Can you take me to Borderlands Market before the sun drops behind the Murky Mountains?"

He said tremblingly, "If I was at home, I would like to, certainly, oh yes. But I have gone away to a dark place where nostriches are safe from danger."

I had a rootle in my rucksack, then quick as a chick I pulled out his head and popped a sock on it.

So now he has got his nerve up again, ready for riding! More tomorrow.

Yours yeeharly,

Cowboy Wolf

PS maybe it was my sore eyes plus dusty white fur made the nostrich think I was an old danger, eh? I must write that trick down in my notebook for Yeller, it is a handy 1, Arrrrooo!

Here I am in Borderlands Market sorebottly. I went bong-bong-bong-bong-bongly across Parching Plain on the back of a nostrich's neck all the way. But between the bongs, I said to myself, "I know, Mister Twister likes getting money off people! So praps I will go 2 the market and have a spy round for him, yes?" I have parked my nostrich in the bicycle rack just near the river.

Mum and Dad
The Lair
Murkshire

Now he is pecking up the nice pawful of pebbles I gave him for his supper. I think I will have a curlup myself under a small bench

Little X

Dear Mum and Dad,

Me wunce morely, near the end part of this day.

Soon after sunjumpup, I woke up thinking. "Wait! Sposing I do see fur and fluff of that fox! He is so crafty he might see me 1st. What shall I dress up as?" Ding came an idea, so I jumped splashingly in the river to get my dust off, then I fluffed up my fur and popped my woggle and my toggle on my neck for a collar. Then off I went wee-pant, wee-pant by many a lampost saying "wuff wuff" (me, not the lamppost, yes?) I was

feeling a bit starving but not for long because of all the people going, "Ahhhhh, nice puppy, pat-pat, have a doggychock."

It was nice, but when I was near the marketplace, guess what? Across the road I ran swiftly, not looking. All of a suddenly, a loud

EEEEEK! came to my ears from a van. Oh no, it was trying to kill me dead!

The old lady driving was all upset and nasty 2 me. She showed me her sharp teeth, then waved her fist. Funny, because the hairs on her head were grey, but the hairs  on her fist were red! Then she put her bonnet back on straight and away she went brrrrmmmly. The name on the side of the van was MRS GENTLY'S FURRY BOOT CO. So I said a joke to that van, I said, "Your driver does not look very Gently to me, get it?"

Now I think I must leave this town, it is 2 dangerous for a small cub here.

Yours narrowsqueakly,

Littly

Dear Mum and Dad,

Good thing I parked that nostrich. Do you know Y? Because that Mrs Gently was not a nice old market lady in a bonnet, not at all!

I crept spyingly into the marketplace, hiding among the legs, also behind fruit and veggies. Then I saw a small crowd gathered round the back of a van. I peeped out behind a small herd of onions wonderingly. I heard a soft voice say, "My dears! I observe that many of your feet are clad only in the thinnest of shoes. How will you protect them from the sharp frosts and snows when winter comes? Allow me to recommend my beautiful Bunnyfur Boots. Step up and look into my eyes while I tell you how cheap and cheering they are."

Straight away all the people opened up their purses saying, "Help yourself, dear lady. I must have a pair of those beautiful Bunnyfur Boots! My footwear is so inadequate, ect." And do you know what? I saw that old lady bend down from the back of her van taking all their money! Then the wind blew her dress up at the back showing her gingery tail, plus blowing a sharp smell of pepper up my nose. So I said, "Oh no, it is Mister Twister my Foe! He pinched those furry boots off our rabbits in Frettnin Forest, I bet!"

Yours sherlockly,

Detective Wolf

PS Grrrr, now I will be like spitted out chewy gum in a fox's tail (hard 2 see, hard to shake off).

Treeline, Mountain Track, Middle Slopes,
Outlaw Peak, Beastshire

Dear Mum and Dad,

It is good having a nostrich in desert places, they are fast gallopers. Plus it is good fun going bong-bong ect so you shake your head off nearly. I am tracking Mister Twister. He packed up quick from the market with a big bag of money. Off he went driving his van eastly. He was a fast brrrmer, but not as speedy as a nostrich because of the road being a rough 1. Soon I was sure he was going to Broken Tooth Caves so I pointed my nostrich off the road. I wanted to go round the back (a bit northly) then climb up Outlaw Peak to have a fine lookout place for my SPOBBs.

When the path started being 2 hilly for my nostrich, off his neck I jumped. I let him keep my sock for his shyness (saves looking for holes), plus I let him eat my woggle, my toggle my foggle and my joggle to stop

95

his tummy going rumble. He said humbly, "Good bye, nice carrying you, you are very fierce but fair."

Up the steep track I went puffingly, keeping a sharp smellout all on my ownly for wolfscent or bearpong plus looking for secret signs. It was not long before I came to some low trees and yessss! A secret sign! It was a sort of a bird, like a fat chicken or a small nostrich maybe. Then  came a shocking SMACK on my head by a low branch. So I thought, "Now I know what that secret sign means. It does not mean 'Chickens coming' or 'Do you like nostriches?' No, it means 'DUCK!'" (Normus is a fine trout tickler but he is rubbish at pics.)

That is all for now,

Yours seeingstarsly,

Bonkhead Boy

Dear Mum and Dad,

My next secret sign that I found was this.

I found where the track turned just under a cliff, like a high wall. I went Grrrrr because of its cheek for meaning 'You are a small weaky, you are like bubbles'. But I found out all of a suddenly it was not a rude sign, because an echo made my GRRRRRR come back very loud 4 times, plus a load of rocks (lairsize) came roaring avalanchely. Lucky I fell flat or no head left! That was how I found out what that sign means really. It means **'SSSSSSSHHH! AVALANCHES!'** (Boo shame.)

I did a short note in my notebook for more secret tracking sign practiss, then up I went more steeply with my eyes going flick, in case of more danger. The next secret sign was more true. It was like this.

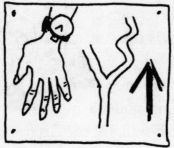

It meant, 'Watch it, take the wiggly path going right', so I did. And it was a good 1, so well done you SPOBBs!

I have just stopped for a short pant and a letter.

Yours reportingly,

Little

Dear Mum and Dad,

Arrroooo! I have found 2 SPOBBs at last.
After a dark, cold, lone walk to the top of Outlaw
Peak, up the other side they came strugglingly!

Yeller whispered loudly,
"HELLO, PL! NORMUS AND
ME HAVE NOT FOUND MISTER
TWISTER BUT WE HAVE MADE A FINE
DISCOVERY!"

I said, "Well done, Yeller. Did you find Spoiler
and Smells?"

He said replyingly, "NO, BUT DID YOU
DETECT MISTER TWISTER?"

I said, "Do not fret and frown, I saw him at Borderlands Market. He will be coming here soonly, I bet. Tell me about the fine discovery you made."

So Yeller said, "WE SEARCHED ALL ROUND BROKEN TOOTH CAVES, SNEAKIN AND PEEKIN IN MANY A DARK TUNNEL, AND DODGIN MANY A CRAFTY TRAP. THEN AT LAST WE FOUND **THE DEN!**"

Normus said addingly, "Yeah, but shame that crafty fox was not at home. I wanted to bash him. What was he doing at Borderlands Market?"

So I said about Mrs Gently selling furry boots ect and Normus said, "Aha! So that was why he wanted those bunnies from Frettnin Forest, to bash them and pinch their fur."

Yeller shouted another Aha saying, "THAT EXPLAINS THE TRICK RABBICK HOLE WE FOUND DOWN BELOW BY MISTER TWISTER'S DEN. A NOTICE OUTSIDE SAYS 'FREE CARROTS'. HOP IN FOR A NIBBLE'. AT FIRST IT LOOKED JUST LIKE ANY OLD BURROW, BUT WHEN WE PEEPED IN WITH OUR TORCHES GOIN FLASH, WE SAW LOADS AND LOADS OF RABBICKS ALL IN SACKS, PEEPIN OUT BLINKINLY."

I said (Pack Leader voice), "SPOBBS, pay attention. It is our job to let those rabbits go. We must send them back to Frettnin Forest where they belong. They need their own holes to pop into. Also, it is not fair them being chased by strangers. They want to be chased by us locals, so they can be normal rabbit pies, not furry boots."

So down we went rushingly to that trick hole. We unsacked the rabbits and sent them back home scamperingly to Frettnin Forest.

Yours fairly,

Little

PS Now we must shut our eyes and think skweezingly about what is keeping Mr Twister from coming back 2 his den. Also, has Stubbs found Spoiler and Smells yet?

Dear Mum and Dad,

Woke up this morning, our tent all white with snow because so highup (snow is Yeller's worst thing, it makes him tremble). But after a warm cookup on our fire (stones all round to stop flames spreading, hem hem) we heard a flippy flap plus a long lost "Ark" that made us all more cheery wunce morely. It was Stubbs!

He said "Ark!" meaning Hark, could we hear the engine of Spoiler's Mobilair that he had been following? Answer, Yes! So out with our fire, down with our tent and off we all crawled peepingly through the sharp white grasses, down the side of the mountain. Way below we saw Broken Tooth Caves plus down further in the valley, the road going wiggle. The snow did not reach there so the Mobilair went nippingly. It was like a small toy bus, stopping close by the turnoff to the caves.

Out jumped Spoiler plus Smells having a piggy back. Also all the Really Harshies. Then we heard a brrrm-pop-pop-bang coming the other way. It sounded like Uncle after he'd eaten all the bakebeans, but it was Mister Twister with engine-trouble! That was Y he was going along creepingly like a snail.

Quick as chicks, the RHYWP made a pretend avalanche and blocked the road by a bend so Mister Twister's van had to stop. Then guess what? They did an ambush and captured him! Yes, true, honest! Mister Twister got captured and *not* by the SPOBBs, so shaming!

Yours shockedly,

L Wolf

Dear Mum and Dad,

This is me. I am hiding in the bushes with the
SPOBBTHALOFs outside the lectric fence
round Spoiler's Mobilair. Sad to say, there is no
way in for us yet.

The RHYWP is a big showoff, singing loud
ambush songs like:

Mister Twister's in a box,
He is just a weaky fox.
Fame is what we all will win,
When we go and turn him in!

He was such a Smartypaw.
He thought he could beat the law!
Spoiler's boys soon put him right.
He will make us rich tonight!

Oh Yah, so Smart are we!
The Really Harsh Young WP!
We came we saw, and then we scored.
Now we get a fat reward!

PUSH! PUSH! AMBUSH!

Then they had to stop because of Smells, you know what he is like when he gets jealous of not getting patted. He opened up the engine cover of the Mobilair and got in with his little hammer, playing **Bonk all the Bits**.

Spoiler said, "I say, stop, Smellybreff! Stop *right now* or you will break it, OK yah?" So Smells said, "Only if you call me Big Fur."

So Spoiler said, "OK, Big Fur, but no bashing engines, alright?"

Then Smells said, "Piggyback, piggyback piggyback piggyback." He did not stop till he made all the RHYWP give him a good bouncy ride. Then he did a sick, saying, "Mummy Mummy."

We want to uncapture him quick, but 2 dangerous yet because of lectric shocks plus large guards.

Yours chewpenly,

Dear Mum and Dad,

Today Yeller had 1 of his best Big Ideas ever, it is called the Trojan Moose! So we gathered all grass plus twiggy stuff plus bits of string, then Stubbs got busy with his clever beak. He knitted a big huge moose like this with a trick door in it, plus room for Normus to hide in.

This is our new plan.

1. Give the RHYWP a big shock by Normus
2. Pinch Mister Twister off Spoiler
3. Uncapture smells
4. Claim huge reward for Mister Twister
5. Get back the proud name of Wolf and say "Well done you SPOBBS!"

When the sun hid behind the Dark Hills, we pushed the Trojan Moose on his wheels and left him outside the lectric fence of the RHYWP camp.

When we got near the Mobilair, we could hear Smells inside talking to Spoiler. Spoiler was trying to have a zizz so they had a little chat starting with Smells:

"Spoiler?"

"OK yah, Big Fur. What do you want?"

"Spoiler?"

"Yah?"

"Spoiler?"

"What do you want?"

"Spoiler?" ect.

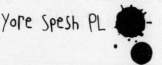

Good, eh? That means he has not changed 1 bit since he went off to be a mascot. He is still ~~a~~ ~~noosance~~ ~~nuisince~~ newsen his normal painy self.

Yours waitingly,

Yore Spesh PL

Dear Mum and Dad,

At Sunjumpup today, us SPOBBs were
listening from our hidyplaces. When we heard the
RHYWP guards
talking, all our eyes
went peep.

The guards said
headscratchingly, "Hey,
what is that? Looks like
some cool statue type
thing, huh? Be careful
man, yah? Leave it
maybe. Could be a
threat, what d'you think?
Check it out with Spoiler,
right, yah?" ect.

Then we heard Smells saying tantrumly, "No!
Me want it! Big Fur want to play wid da moosy!"

Spoiler came out of the Mobilair yawningly,
saying, "Oh bring it in, it's only some big toy. Let
Smellybreff play with it, for howling out loud!
Anything's better than having to play **Ga Ga Goo**

again, yah?" So the guards turned off the lectric, and pushed the Trojan Moose inside the fence.

Soon Smells was more cheery playing **Gee up Moosy to the Fair**, plus making all the guards say, "Giddy Up Big Fur!"

Stubbs said a whisper "Ark!" meaning *Ark*splain what **Ga Ga Goo** is. So I said 2 him how it is 1 of Smells's best games. He has to be the Mummy with the lipstick, then you have to lie down and be the Big Baby and let him feed you mud stew by a bottle.

Now it is getting late, Yeller me and Stubbs are a bit wurrid, case Normus gets bashed or captured by all the strong Harshies. What if they all gang up on him? Will he get the biggest Chinese burn ever?

Your nervous,

Number 1 Cub

Dear Mum and Dad,

Whyo Y did I fret and frown about Normus?
He is a mighty hero and a Big Shocker!

1st he waited till Smells got bored of **Gee Up
Moosy**. That was when Smells said, "Who wants
to play **Doctors** and baggsie me do
injeckshuns!" Then all the guards went away
zoomingly to hide behind the Mobilair.

Quick as a chick, out jumped
Normus with a big
GROWL! He ripped
the front wheel off the
Mobilair. That gave all
the Harshies a nasty
shock so they packed
together showing their
sharp teeth. Then they
shouted "PUSH!
PUSH! AMBUSH!"
Spoiler was in the front
of the attack, all bristly
and big as a buffalo!

But Normus was not scared 1 bit. He closed 1 eye
and rolled that tyre bowlingly at them. That made
them turn the other way sharp! They all went,
"HELP! HELP! WIPE-OUT! Then they went
BOING over the lectric fence like scaredy kangaroos.

Me and Yeller were waiting on the other side
with Mister Twister's rabbit sacks and in the
Harshies went plop plop plop plop! They could not
get out again because Stubbs tied them up quick
with spesh SPOBB ~~nkots nots~~ knots by his clever
beak! Spoiler wanted to jump the fence like the
rest of the RHYWP but he was the last 1. That is Y
he got squished by a front tyre bowling him over,
shame, eh? Not really, ARRRRRRROOOOO!

Now I 'spect his mum will say, "What Ho you
flat young cowpat, have you seen our darling
grate big harsh cub called Spoiler?" And he will
say, "Blub blub Mummy, it is me."

Yours speshly,

ARkela of SPOBBS (Stubbs idea)

113

Dear Mum and Dad,

Just a short letter today because of being busy with our prisoners. We are keeping Spoiler in the lickroom of the captured Mobilair. He is coming unsquished in a slow way, so looking like his normal beautiful hansum self (only kidding, not really).

Mister Twister is still captured 2. BUT (big but) we cannot claim our huge reward because he is in the secret cell and Spoiler will not say the combination of the secret panel to me, boo shame! Spoiler keeps saying smarmly, "I say, listen up Little Wolf. Y don't we PLs just agree to split the large reward for arresting Mister Twister? I mean, isn't that fairnuff, yah? Look here, you just release me and my pack, then I will give you the combination and we can all go along to the police station and get really really wealthy. Sound plan, yah?"

Yours notsurewhattodonextly,

Little

PS Smells is fine only he keeps snuggling up to Spoiler's door going "Numb-ah numb-ah numb-ah numb-ah." Just because he wants to see Mister Twister and say "Nar Nar" 2 him I bet.

Dear Mum and Dad,

Do not go mad and get your temper up, but Mister Twister has done a fast getaway. This is how.

Me, Yeller and Stubbs were outside the Mobilair watching Normus bash the wheel back on the front. Smells came down the steps of the Mobilair with eyes wide as windows plus big naughty smile. Also he was hiding something behind his back. He looked at Normus in a crafty way. "Have you put da wheel back on, Normus?" Then Normus said, eyerollingly, "Yes, Smells, this round thing is the wheel. It is not off any more. That is cos of me bashing it back ON, is that clear?"

Then, all of a rushly, Mister Twister popped up behind Smells and pushed him off the steps! He shut the driver's door of the Mobilair thuddingly. Then he started up the engine, shouting, "Such a pity my boys! I must leave you in a hurry. Consider yourselves OUTFOXED!" Then off he went screechingly, going beep beep, dustcloud dustcloud.

All of us SPOBBs did a pretend sob and waved byebye. Then we jumped upanddownly, doing our pack Arrroooo! times 3 for cheeryness!

Yours hi5ly,

L Wolf

PS I forgot to say about Stubbs going "Ark" meaning Arksplain what you are hiding behind your back, smells. Answer, moneybag moneybag moneybag, mine mine mine!

Dear Mum and Dad,

Thank you for your present of a large empty shoebox plus string so Smells can make a nice parcel and send all his money to you. Yes, I will ask nicely but you know what a big miser he is.

You say in your note, "Say fine work to him and kiss his darling fluffy cheeks for Mummy." Plus you say to me, "Never darken our lair door again, also deliver yourself a sharp clip round the hearole for going barmy. You are hopeless and have let down our proud name of Wolf, as usual, while giving the Snarl-Wolfingtons loads to sneer about!"

But Mum and Dad, Y are you so crool? You do not understand! Mister Twister was not the winner! Listen, I will tell you the score, it is:

MISTER Twister, NIL
SPOBBTHALOFS 999999999 millium
Spoiler plus RHYWP, NIL
SPOBBTHALOFS 9999999 millium
milliums

But you will not even listen how we did it , I
bet, so I am all upset. Plus I am going home with
a stampy stamp.

Your sulkingly,

Not Telling

Dear Mum and Dad,

Aha! I can see from your gloating note saying, "Arrrooooo and Nar Nar, the Snarl-Wolfingtons have done a moonlight flit with their tails between their legs," that you are feeling a lot more cheery today!

So merci (French) for writing, also for Dad's spy-photo of Mister Twister's letter that he sent to them.

Dear Mr and Mrs Snarl-Wolfington,

I have recently turned the tables on your precious Spoiler by single-handedly capturing him and his entire pack of Really Harsh Young Wolves. They surrendered to me without a struggle and I have them all tied up in sacks in their fine Mobilair that I have confiscated to replace my old van. Harsh? I have known frogspawn harsher than your son.

May I suggest that you sell your mansion immediately and send the money you get for it to me? I feel sure that you will wish to do this speedily before your neighbours, Grizzle and Gripper find out what a complete mess your only cub made of his attempt to capture me and become famous.

Yours smugly,

Mister Twister the Fox

Also, Mum and Dad, you say you are grrring to know how this arrrooooooey thing happened. Oh all right, then, I will tell you a nice story. It is called "How Little Wolf, Pack Leader of the SPOBBs beat Spoiler plus Mister Twister in 1 go." Ready?

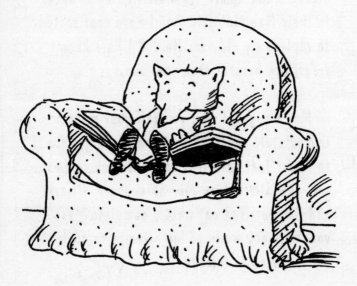

How Little Wolf, Pack Leader of the SPOBBs Beat Spoiler plus Mister Twister in 1 Go.
By L Wolf.

Wunce upon a Mobilair there was a very small bad cub called Smells. He was always getting on everywun's nerves going, "Numb-ah numb-ah numb-ah numb-ah" ect, all the time in people's ears. Well, do you know a funny thing? There was a grate huge posh cub called Spoiler Snarl-Wolfington

who was PL of the RHWYP. He had grate big sharp teeth and all big mussels. BUT (big but) he was not like Little Wolf and his SPOBBs who were used to Smells going on and on. So after only about ten hours Spoiler gave in saying, "Please, I'll do anything you want, OK yah?" So Smells made him whisper the combination of his secret cell to him.

Then Smells's hansum big bruv Little Wolf guessed something was up, so he said, "Come on baby bruv, what did  Spoiler whisper? You can tell me, you are in my pack really." But Smells just shook his head going ppppppppppprrrr with his lips.

So Little Wolf found out the answer in a very crafty way. First he did a whisper to Normus saying, "Normus, you go and bash the wheel back on the Mobilair." Then Little Wolf did another whisper to Yeller (his best friend and cuz) saying, "Go and put the Mobilair driving keys in the driving keyhole." Then Little Wolf went, "Psss wsss ect," in Stubbs's hearole just to make Smells jealous.

Smells said, "Give ME a whisper!" So Little Wolf said, "OK, Big Fur, I will." He whispered to him, "Whatever you do, you must never never never stand outside the secret door and say to Mr Twister, "Hello in there. If you give me your bag of money, I will open the door to the secret room by a secret combination."

And Smells said replyingly, "OK I promise." Then off he trotted gigglingly with his paw over his smile.

Straightaway, off the Mobilair jumped Little Wolf, Pack Leader plus the SPOBBs. They did not have to wait long before OUT came Smells with his eyes wide as windows hiding the moneybag behind his back. Then off drove Little Wolf's foxy foe in the Mobilair with Spoiler plus the RHYWP in the back!

Yours happyeverafterly,

The Storyteller

Dear Mum and Dad,

We are packing up our Pack Tent today and getting ready to go back to Frettnin Forest for a proper old-fashy rabbit hunt. Arrrrroooo!

Our sleep last night was the longest yet, hmm nice, because Smells wanted to have his sleep in the Trojan Moose, handy eh? He helped us get ready (in a way) by chewing through all the guy ropes before we woke up.

Can you send him a photo of Dad saying "No weeing on fires?" We had to have our potty noodles a bit cold today all because of Smells liking the sound of HISSSSS. (Never mind, xtra rations of bakebeans to make up, I love them kiss kiss.)

Yours goinghomely,

ittle

Comfy Armchair

Dear Mum and Dad,

Thank you for your letter saying well done in teeny small letters, I know it hurt.

Dad says he does not understand Y we did not just drive Mister Twister to the Police and claim the huge reward like any normal wolf would have done.

Answer (in Yeller's words, the same wuns he said to Normus when he asked that kwestion) "YES, BUT WHAT A BIG SHAME IF WE TAKE HIM TO THE PLEECE. THEN WE WON'T HAVE ANY PROPER ENEMIES IN FRETTNIN FOREST AND THAT IS NOT RIGHT, LICKLE!

WHERE IS THE CHALLENGE FOR US
SPOBBS IF OUR BEST CRAFTY FOE IS
AWAY BEIN A CONVICT?"

See? We like crafty foes to
help us sharpen up our tricks!

Now I will say cheero, I am off to chase rabbits,
also to stuff wool up my ears. Did I say that Smells
made me send off Mister Twister's moneybag for a
drum kit? I was hoping he would find a nice quiet
craze instead of being a drummer in a pop band,
but no luck. All because of Mister Twister saying
he was a star, just for opening the door of his
secret cell, boo shame.

Yours deffly,

WOlf PACK IT IN LEADER!